"What's the Matter with Andrew?"

A guide to understanding children with Autism

Kim Walsh-Solio

Published by Tate Publishing & Enterprises, LLC
127 E. Trade Center Terrace | Mustang, Oklahoma 73064 USA
1.888.361.9473 | www.tatepublishing.com

Tate Publishing is committed to excellence in the publishing industry. The company reflects the philosophy established by the founders, based on Psalm 68:11,
"The Lord gave the word and great was the company of those who published it."

Book design copyright © 2015 by Tate Publishing, LLC. All rights reserved.
Cover and interior design by Cecille Kaye Gumadan
Illustrations by JZ Sagario

Published in the United States of America

ISBN: 978-1-63268-694-7
Juvenile Nonfiction / Social Issues / Special Needs
14.11.28

To Andrew. Thanks for being born. Love, Mom.

Preface

Dear Reader,

When Andrew was about sixteen months old he started to gaze off and wasn't responding to his name. At first, we thought he may be deaf, so we had his hearing checked. The test came back negative, "what a relief Andrew could hear!" but still, in the deep inner part of myself, I knew "something" was wrong. Andrew wasn't "just" a difficult to soothe baby and oh boy did he cry A LOT! It wasn't until months later that a visit to my brothers house would help shed some light on "what's the matter with Andrew." My sister in-law had worked with special-needs children, and she had noticed that some of Andrew's behaviors were "red flags," so to speak. My brother called me the next day to kindly tell me "Keri thinks Andrew has PDD, pervasive development delay." He assured me that with the right treatment, most children make great gains. So with a referral to Dr. Karen Levine, who at the time was from Building Blocks, we received a diagnosis of autism for Andrew at eighteen months of age in 2004. AUTISM! The only reference I had to autism was the movie Rain Man and that Doug Flutie's son was recently diagnosed with autism. I remembered seeing a picture of him and his family and thinking he doesn't "look" like anything is wrong with him. So from there we began early intervention services; we were receiving therapies including ABA, floor time, occupational therapy, physical therapy, behavioral therapy, speech therapy, and sensory integration. We were coming and going, and Andrew was responding well to our new routine. I sat in on most sessions to educate myself; I read everything I could find in books and online searches. I knew it was going to be a long hard road, but I was determined Andrew would speak. I had read about the "window" that if a child did not speak by the age of six, they probably would not speak at all. As difficult and draining as it was, I spent every waking moment prompting Andrew to use his words combined with sign language. It took one solid year to get him to say "for me" as I hand over hand tapped his little chest over and over and over again! Holding the spoon horizontally was another challenge, as Andrew would hold the spoon upright and all the food would drop down, resulting in meltdowns and tantrums. But yet again, hand over hand for what seemed like an eternity, he finally mastered the art of the spoon. Using a straw was another hurdle, as well as giving kisses with a smooch instead of a open mouth slobber. We received early intervention services until Andrew was three years old. The day after his third birthday he started school full-time, and I was suddenly handing over my child for six hours a day, five days a week. I found myself feeling very isolated and alone, no longer involved with the therapies Andrew was receiving. Then one day while sitting in my car waiting for Andrew to get out of school, I started to write down my thoughts on a napkin that seemed to be downloading into me and would eventually end up on the pages of What's the Matter with Andrew. As I navigated through my new world called autism, the years went by—it has been 9 1/2 years since Andrew's diagnosis and the road has been long and hard, but the rewards were so worth it. Andrew has found his way and is verbal today; he loves to make animations on his computer, and I encourage him to do so. I don't remember life before this journey began when I took for granted that children were born "typical." I now understand that God works in mysterious ways, and autism is a great mystery. These children are special and have a purpose in this world. They say Albert Einstein was autistic and to be completely honest I think we all are on some level. Autism is a spectrum and there is a large umbrella that each individual child falls under. High functioning autistic is what Andrew is considered, meaning he can blend in with most children until an episode or tantrum exposes him as "different." There is no known cure for autism, just coping mechanisms we learn as we go. Therapies certainly do help but, we the parents have the brunt of the responsibility to bring the child out of the cocoon of autism and into our world. Never give up on your child he/she is here for a purpose. May God bless you as you figure out what your child's purpose is.

Acknowledgments

I would like to acknowledge all the wonderful, professional men and women who have worked with Andrew beginning with Dr. Karen Levine, the psychologist who diagnosed Andrew in 2004; Early Intervention Services from Building Blocks and Tri-City; the Malden Public Schools, especially the Special Ed Department; Shore Collaborative; and Futures Clinic. Without all your hard work and dedication, Andrew would not be where he is today. Thanks to our family who supported us as we were challenged on a daily basis. To our church, Trinity Evangelical in N. Reading, Massachusetts, where we were accepted and prayed for. To my mother, who believed in me and gave me the money needed to get this book published. To Jenni and Robert, for always accepting Andrew and loving him and all his quirkiness. To God, for blessing me with such a special child and Andrew Thomas Solio for being born; I'm so proud to be your mom.

Andrew is a little boy who looks like you and me, but Andrew is different. What could it be?

Andrew is a child with Autism.

Autism, what could that be?

Autism is a neurological disorder, which means their brains are wired differently; think of a computer.

Autism affects what is known as sensory integration, which simply means the way their bodies process physical sensations: lights, sounds, touch and speech. it even affects the way they eat.

Because Andrew is autistic he hears both lights and sounds on a higher frequency. The world can be a very scary place.

It is sometimes hard and a bit too much for Andrew to be out in public places. It's hard too for all of you I can see it on your faces.

Andrew may look like he is bad when he has tantrums, cries, and screams, but it's because he feels scared and is sometimes afraid of things.

Just try to imagine how hard it must be for Andrew to get his haircut. People may think it's mean because we have to hold him down while he screams, it must look like human torture!

But what are we to do his hair grows too and I know he'll be fine as soon as it's over.

Andrew has trouble using his words and out of frustration he may screech, but it's not because he doesn't know, he just can't use his speech!

People might think that he cannot hear well; if you call his name he may not look. But it's not because he's trying to ignore you. He would answer if he could.

There are learning delays we have to contend with, so it's not easy getting through. That is why we have to repeat things hoping eventually for a breakthrough.

I don't think we understand exactly what he's thinking, but all I know is he is aware of everything he's seeking!

His teacher says she thinks he'll read and he has a lot of skills. Concentration comes real easy, he has a super focused will!

We might find him staring at his trains for hours and hours. He's quite the artist and he loves singing; his screams reach rock star status.

They say he has no sense of self. Autism has no ego. So if that's true his soul's pure too, no wonder he's my angel.-

My son Andrew is truly happy, I can see it in his smile. For it is there that I'm aware God's love is in my child!

I have been told he is not aware of his body as in space. Perhaps it's because he is after all "of a heavenly place."

So what's the matter with Andrew? You might ask if you see him on the streets. But as I say, "He was born the way God had meant for him to be!"

As his mom I'm here to tell you there's a genius trapped inside. It is there. I am aware. I can see it in his eyes.

Autism is still a mystery to the medical community. It strikes all walks of life. No race has an immunity.-

There is no known cure for Autism but Autism awareness leads to early intervention which is the best chance these children have to help them overcome the challenges of everyday life. Look for the red flags that usually appear around 16-18 months of age.

- Loss of any skills

- Developmental delays

- Little to no speech

- Echolalia

- Little to no eye contact

- At times appears deaf

- Repetitive movements

- Lines things up

- Spins things to stare at

- Walks on toes

- Flapping of arms

- Sensitivity to lights and sounds

- Afraid of things for no apparent reason

- Lots of screaming for what appears to be nothing

- Stares at fans and other moving objects

- Meltdowns/tantrums

- Sleeplessness/night terrors

- Appears to be in their own world

If you suspect Autism contact your doctor and your local school district. You are your child's advocate. It's your voice that needs to be heard.

Autism is a condition affecting the processing, integrating and organizing of information that significantly impacts communication, social interactions, functional skills and educational performance. There are many manifestations and degrees of severity within the Autism Spectrum.

e|LIVE

listen|imagine|view|experience

AUDIO BOOK DOWNLOAD INCLUDED WITH THIS BOOK!

In your hands you hold a complete digital entertainment package. In addition to the paper version, you receive a free download of the audio version of this book. Simply use the code listed below when visiting our website. Once downloaded to your computer, you can listen to the book through your computer's speakers, burn it to an audio CD or save the file to your portable music device (such as Apple's popular iPod) and listen on the go!

How to get your free audio book digital download:

1. Visit www.tatepublishing.com and click on the e|LIVE logo on the home page.
2. Enter the following coupon code:
   b426-42e0-e25d-857e-c10e-dd4b-ae85-9d1b
3. Download the audio book from your e|LIVE digital locker and begin enjoying your new digital entertainment package today!